A LOOK AT SPACE SCIENCE

BLACK HOLES

BY BERT WILBERFORCE

Gareth Stevens PUBLISHING

Please visit our website, www.garethstevens.com. For a free color catalog of all our high-quality books, call toll free 1-800-542-2595 or fax 1-877-542-2596.

Library of Congress Cataloging-in-Publication Data
Names: Wilberforce, Bert, author.
Title: Black holes / Bert Wilberforce.
Description: New York : Gareth Stevens Publishing, [2021] | Series: A look at space science | Includes bibliographical references and index. | Contents: Black holes are real! -- What is it? -- Einstein's idea -- From star to black hole -- How many? -- Finding the invisible -- Big and bigger -- Around and around -- The event horizon -- More to discover -- Three kinds of black holes.
Identifiers: LCCN 2019040017 | ISBN 9781538259429 (paperback) | ISBN 9781538259436 (6 pack) | ISBN 9781538259443 (library binding) | ISBN 9781538259450 (ebook)
Subjects: LCSH: Black holes (Astronomy)--Juvenile literature.
Classification: LCC QB843.B55 W55 2021 | DDC 523.8/875--dc23
LC record available at https://lccn.loc.gov/2019040017

First Edition

Published in 2021 by
Gareth Stevens Publishing
111 East 14th Street, Suite 349
New York, NY 10003

Designer: Sarah Liddell
Editor: Therese Shea

Photo credits: Cover, p. 1 (main) Vadim Sadovski/Shutterstock.com; background used throughout Zakharchuk/Shutterstock.com; p. 5 Lonely/Shutterstock.com; p. 7 andrey_l/Shutterstock.com; p. 9 (main) vchal/Shutterstock.com; p. 9 (Einstein) Triggerhippie4/Wikimedia Commons; p. 11 vector-map/Shutterstock.com; p. 13 CahekZ/Shutterstock.com; p. 15 Harbingerdawn/Wikimedia Commons; p. 17 Maxal Tamor/Shutterstock.com; p. 19 Sergey Nivens/Shutterstock.com; p. 21 Marc Ward/Shutterstock.com; p. 23 Artsiom Petrushenka/Shutterstock.com; p. 25 Ixocactus/Wikimedia Commons; p. 27 BevinKacon/Wikimedia Commons; p. 29 GDK/Wikimedia Commons.

Printed in the United States of America

CPSIA compliance information: Batch #CS20GS: For further information contact Gareth Stevens, New York, New York at 1-800-542-2595.

CONTENTS

Words in the glossary appear in **bold** type the first time they are used in the text.

BLACK HOLES ARE REAL!

Black holes are often in TV shows and movies about space. These places in outer space suck in anything that gets too close. They make stories about space **exciting**! Black holes are real, not make-believe. Scientists learn more about them every day.

MAKE THE GRADE

Scientists proved that black holes are real in 1994.

HOW IT WORKS

A black hole has a very powerful force of **gravity**. It draws in all matter that gets close. It even draws in light! Because it does this, it appears black. But it's really invisible, or unable to be seen.

MAKE THE GRADE

Scientist John Wheeler gave black holes their name because of their dark appearance.

EINSTEIN'S IDEA

In 1915, scientist Albert Einstein presented an idea about gravity in space. He said objects with great **mass** bend space and time much more than objects with less mass. They have a strong force of gravity too. His idea meant a black hole was possible.

MAKE THE GRADE

Einstein's idea was called the general theory of relativity.

An object that has enough gravity to trap light is also very, very dense. That means the bits of matter that it's made of are tightly packed together. Large stars can become objects like this if they collapse, or cave in.

MAKE THE GRADE

Our sun has a lot of mass, but not enough to become a black hole.

FROM STAR TO BLACK HOLE

Many stars are much larger than our sun. While a large star is burning, it stays about the same size. When there's nothing left to burn, the star can collapse under its own gravity. It can become a black hole.

MAKE THE GRADE

A star needs to be more than three times the mass of our sun to become a black hole.

HOW MANY?

Scientists think there may be as many as 10 **million** or even a **billion** black holes just in our **galaxy**, the Milky Way. Since black holes are invisible, scientists have come up with special ways to find them.

MILKY WAY GALAXY

MAKE THE GRADE

It can take billions of years for a star to burn out and become a black hole.

FINDING THE INVISIBLE

We see objects when light **reflects** off them. Since black holes suck in light, we can't see them. However, scientists can see the effects that black holes have on objects near them. That's how they know black holes are there!

MAKE THE GRADE

Black holes may be at the center of every galaxy.

As matter gets sucked into a black hole, it gives off energy, or power, called X-rays. We can't see X-rays, but certain special machines can find them. In 1971, a satellite spotted a black hole by finding X-rays near it.

MAKE THE GRADE

A satellite is a machine sent into space that moves around an object in space such as Earth or the sun.

SATELLITE

BIG AND BIGGER

Different sizes of black holes have different names. Stellar black holes are up to 20 times the mass of our sun. The largest black holes are called supermassive black holes. They're more massive than 1 million suns!

MAKE THE GRADE

"Stellar" means "having to do with stars."

AROUND AND AROUND

Not all matter near a black hole gets sucked into it right away. Some matter, like gas and dust, **orbits** the black hole. The matter forms what's called an accretion (uh-KREE-shun) disk. Matter may fall into the black hole if a force moves it closer.

MAKE THE GRADE

Gravity is the force that keeps objects in orbit. Gravity keeps Earth in orbit around the sun.

ACCRETION DISK

THE EVENT HORIZON

In 2017, scientists found a black hole using the Event Horizon **Telescope**. This isn't just one telescope, however. It's many telescopes working together to find waves of energy called radio waves. These telescopes are called radio telescopes because they find radio waves.

= EVENT HORIZON TELESCOPE STATION

MAKE THE GRADE

An event horizon is the point at which nothing can escape from a black hole's gravity.

The Event Horizon Telescope used the **data** from eight telescopes to put together the first ever picture of a black hole. It was a supermassive black hole in the center of a faraway galaxy called M87.

MAKE THE GRADE

The Event Horizon Telescope picture doesn't show the black hole itself. It shows the matter around the black hole.

MORE TO DISCOVER

Scientists once thought there were two black hole sizes. Now they know there are more. They also think black holes join together to make supermassive black holes. Tools like the Chandra X-ray **Observatory** will help scientists find new data and new black holes!

CHANDRA X-RAY OBSERVATORY

MAKE THE GRADE

Scientists have learned that black holes create wind and can blow matter away at high speeds.

THREE KINDS OF BLACK HOLES

NAME	SIZE	MASS
primordial	about the size of an atom	as much as a large mountain
stellar	about the size of a ball 10 miles (16 km) across	up to 20 times the mass of the sun
supermassive	about the size of a ball as big as our **solar system**	greater than 1 million times the mass of the sun

GLOSSARY

billion: 1,000 million, or 1,000,000,000

data: facts and figures

exciting: causing feelings of great interest

galaxy: a large group of stars, planets, gas, and dust that form a unit within the universe

gravity: the force that pulls objects toward the center of a planet, star, or another place in space

mass: the amount of matter in an object

million: a thousand thousands, or 1,000,000

observatory: a special building or satellite from which scientists watch the sky and study weather and space

orbit: to travel in a circle or oval around something, or the path used to make that trip

reflect: to give back light

solar system: the sun and all the space objects that orbit it, including the planets and their moons

telescope: a tool that makes faraway objects look bigger and closer

FOR MORE INFORMATION

BOOKS

Latta, Sara. *Black Holes: The Weird Science of the Most Mysterious Objects in the Universe*. Minneapolis, MN: Twenty-First Century Books, 2017.

Roland, James. *Black Holes: A Space Discovery Guide*. Minneapolis, MN: Lerner Publications, 2017.

WEBSITES

Black Holes
www.ducksters.com/science/black_hole.php
Read more about these powerful forces.

Black Holes
www.esa.int/kids/en/learn/Our_Universe/Story_of_the_Universe/Black_Holes
Find out how the European Space Agency explains black holes.

INDEX